Young Robin Hood

G. Manville Fenn

Contents

YOUNG ROBIN HOOD

BY

G. Manville Fenn

CHAPTER I

Sit still, will you? I never saw such a boy: wriggling about like a young eel."

"I can't help it, David," said the little fellow so roughly spoken to by a sour-looking serving man; "the horse does jog so, and it's so slippery. If I didn't keep moving I should go off."

"You'll soon go off if you don't keep a little quieter," growled the man angrily, "for I'll pitch you among the bushes."

"No, you won't," said the boy laughing. "You daren't do so."

"What! I'll let you see, young master. I want to know why they couldn't let you have a donkey or a mule, instead of hanging you on behind me."

"Aunt said I should be safer behind you," said the boy; "but I'm not. It's so hard to hold on by your belt, because you're so----"

"Look here. Master Robin, I get enough o' that from the men. If you say I'm so fat, I'll pitch you into the first patch o' brambles we come to."

"But you are fat," said the boy; "and you dare not. If you did my father would punish you."

"He wouldn't know."

"Oh! yes he would, David," said the little fellow, confidently; "the other men would tell him."

"They wouldn't know," said the man with a chuckle. "I say, aren't you afraid?"

"No," said the boy. "What of, tumbling off? I could jump."

"'Fraid of going through this great dark forest?"

"No. What is there to be afraid of?"

"Robbers and thieves, and all sorts of horrid things. Why, we might meet Robin Hood and his men."

"I should like that," said the boy.

"What?" cried the serving man, and he looked round at the great oak and beech trees through which the faintly marked road lay, and then forward and backward at the dozen mules, laden with packs of cloth, every two of which were led by an armed man. "You'd like that?"

"Yes," said the boy. "I want to see him."

"Here's a pretty sort of a boy," said the man. "Why, he'd eat you like a radish."

"No, he wouldn't," said the boy, "because I'm not a bit like a radish; and I say, David, do turn your belt round."

"Turn my belt round?" said the man, in astonishment. "What for?"

"So as to put the sword the other side. It does keep on banging my legs so. They're quite bruised."

"It's me that'll be bruised, with you punching and sticking your fisties into my belt. Put your legs on the other side. I can't move my sword. I might want it to fight, you know."

"Who with?" asked the boy.

"Robbers after the bales o' cloth. I shall be precious glad to get 'em safe to the town, and be back home again with whole bones. Sit still, will you! Wriggling again! How am I to get you safe home to your father if you keep sidling off like that? Want me to hand you over to one of the men?"

"Yes, please," said the boy, dolefully.

"What? Don't want to ride on one of the mules, do you?"

"Yes, I do," said the boy. "I should be more comfortable sitting on one of the packs. I'm sure aunt would have said I was to sit there, if she had known."

"Look here, young squire," said the man, sourly; "you've too much tongue, and you know too much what aren't good for you. Your aunt, my old missus, says to me:

"'David,' she says, 'you are to take young Master Robin behind you on the horse, where he can hold on by your belt, and you'll never lose sight of him till you give him into his father the Sheriff's hands, along with the bales of cloth; and you can tell the Sheriff he has been a very good boy during his visit'; and now I can't."

"Why can't you?" said the boy, sharply.

"'Cause you're doing nothing but squirming and working about behind my saddle. I shall never get you to the town, if you go on like this."

The boy puckered up his forehead, and was silent as he wondered whether he could manage to sit still for the two hours which were yet to elapse before they stopped for the night at a village on the outskirts of Sherwood Forest, ready to go on again the next morning.

"I liked stopping with aunt at Ellton," said the little fellow to himself, sadly, "and I should like to go again; but I should like to be fetched home next time, for old David is so cross every time I move, and——"

"Look here, young fellow," growled the man, half turning in his saddle; "if you don't sit still I'll get one of the pack ropes and tie you on, like a sack. I never see such a fidgety young elver in my——Oh, look at that!"

The man gave a tug at his horse's rein; but it was not needed, for the stout cob had cocked its ears forward and stopped short, just as the mules in front whisked themselves round, and the men who drove them began to huddle together in a group.

For all at once the way was barred by about a dozen men in rough weather-stained green jerkins, each with a long bow and a sheaf of arrows at his back, and a long quarter-staff in his hand.

David, confidential servant and head man to Aunt Hester, of the cloth works at Ellton, looked sharply round at the half-dozen heavily-laden mules behind him; and beyond them he saw another dozen or so of men, and more were coming from among the trees to right and left.

"Hoi! all of you," cried David to his men. "Swords out! We must fight for the mistress's cloth."

As he spoke, he seized the hilt of his sword and began to tug at it; but it would not leave its sheath, and all the while he was kicking at his horse's ribs with his heels, with the result that the stout cob gave a kick and a plunge, lowered its head, and dashed off at a gallop, with David holding on to the pommel.

Two of the men made a snatch at the reins, but they were too late, and turned to the mule-drivers, who were following their leader's example and trying to escape amongst the trees, leaving the mules huddled together, squealing and kicking in their fright.

Young Robin just saw two packages roll to the ground as the cob dashed off; then he was holding on with all his might to old David's belt as the cob galloped away with half-a-dozen of the robbers trying to cut it off.

Then the little fellow felt that he was being jerked and knocked and bruised, as the horse tore along with David, head and neck stretched out. There was a rush under some low boughs, and another rush over a patch of brambles and tall bracken; then the cob made a bold dash at a dense mass of low growth, when there was a violent jerk as he made a bound, followed by a feeling as if the boy's arms were being torn out at the shoulders, a rush through the air, a heavy blow, and a sensation of tearing, and all was, giddiness and pain.

CHAPTER II

It is not nice to be pitched by a man off a horse's back on to the top of your head.

That is what young Robin thought as he sat up and rubbed the place, looking very rueful and sad.

But he did not seem to be entirely alone there in the dense forest, for there was another young robin, with large eyes and a speckled jacket, sitting upon a twig and watching him intently. Robin could think of nothing but himself, his aching head, and his scratches, some of which were bleeding.

Then he listened, and fancied that he heard shouting, with the trampling of mules and the breaking of twigs.

But he was giddy and puzzled, and after struggling through some undergrowth he sat down upon what looked like a green velvet cushion; but it was only the moss-covered root of a great beech tree, which covered him like a roof and made all soft and shady.

And now it was perfectly quiet, and it seemed restful after being shaken and jerked about on the horse's back. Robin was tired too, and the dull, half-stupefied state of his brain stopped him from being startled by his strange position. His head ached though, and it seemed nice to rest it, and he stretched himself out on the moss and looked up through the leaves of the great tree, where he could see in one place the ruddy rays of the evening sun glowing, and then he could see nothing--think nothing.

Then he could think, though he still could not see, for it was very dark and silent and strange, and for some minutes he could not understand why he was out there on the moss instead of being in Aunt Hester's house at Elton, or at home in Nottingham town.

But he understood it all at once, recollecting what had taken place, and for a time he felt very, very miserable. It was startling, too, when from close at hand someone seemed to begin questioning him strangely by calling out:

"Whoo-who-who-who?"

But at the end of a minute or two he knew it was an owl, and soon after he was fast asleep and did not think again till the sun was shining brightly, and he sat up waiting for old David to come and pull him up on the horse again.

Robin waited, for he was afraid to move.

"If I begin to wander about," he said to himself, "David will not find me, and he will go home and tell father I'm lost, when all the time he threw me off the horse because he was afraid and wanted to save himself."

So the boy sat still, waiting to be fetched. The robin came and looked at him again, as if wondering that he did not pull up flowers by the roots and dig, so that worms and grubs might be found, and finally flitted away.

Then all at once there was the pattering of feet, and half-a-dozen deer came into sight, with soft dappled coats, and one of them with large flat pointed horns; but at the first movement Robin made they dashed off among the trees in a series of bounds.

Then there was another long pause, and Robin was thinking how hungry he was, when something dropped close to him with a loud rap, and looking up sharply, he caught sight of a little keen-eyed bushy-tailed animal, looking down from a great branch as if in search of something it had let fall.

"Squirrel!" said Robin aloud, and the animal heard and saw him at the same moment, showing its annoyance at the presence of an intruder directly. For it began to switch its tail and scold after its fashion, loudly, its utterances seeming like a repetition of the word "chop" more or less quickly made.

Finding its scolding to be in vain, and that the boy would not go, the squirrel did the next best thing--bounded along from bough to bough; while, after waiting wearily in the hope of seeing David, the boy began to look round this tree and the next, and finally made his way some little distance farther into the forest, to be startled at last by a harsh cry which was answered from first one place and then another by the noisy party of jays that had been disturbed in their happy solitude.

To Robin it was just as if the first one had cried "Hoi! I say, here's a boy." And weary with waiting, and hungry as he was, the constant harsh shouting irritated the little fellow so that he hurried away followed by quite a burst of what seemed to be mocking cries, with the intention of finding the track leading across the forest; but he had not gone far before he found himself in an open glade, dotted with beautiful great oak trees, and nearly covered with the broad leaves of the bracken, which were agitated by something passing through and beneath, giving forth a grunting sound. Directly after he caught sight of a long black back, then of others, and he saw that he was close to a drove of small black pigs, hunting for acorns. One of the pigs found him at the same moment and saluted him with a sharp, barking sound wonderfully like that of a dog.

This was taken up directly by the other members of the drove, who with a great deal of barking and grunting came on to the attack, for they did not confine themselves to threatening, their life in the forest making them fierce enough to be dangerous.

Robin's first thought was to run away, but he knew that four legs are better than two for getting over the ground, and felt that the drove would attack him more fiercely if they saw that he was afraid.

His next idea was to climb 'up into the fork of one of the big trees, but he knew that there was not time. So he obeyed his third notion, which was to jump to where a big piece of dead wood lay, pick it up, and hit the foremost pig across the nose with it.

That blow did wonders; it made the black pig which received it utter a dismal squeal, and its companions stop and stand barking and snapping all around him. But the blow broke the piece of dead wood in two, and the fierce little animals were coming on again, when a voice cried:

"Hi! you! knocking our tigs about!" And a rough boy about a couple of years older than Robin rushed into the middle of the herd, kicking first at one and then at another, banging them with a long hooked stick he held, and making them run squealing in all directions. "What are you knocking our tigs about for?" cried the boy sharply, as he stared hard at the strange visitor to the forest, his eyes looking greedily at the little fellow's purple and white jerkin and his cap with a little white feather in it.

"They were coming to bite me," said Robin quickly, while it struck him as funny that the boy should knock the pigs about himself.

"What are you doing here?" said the boy.

Robin told of his misfortune, and finished by saying:

"I'm so hungry, and I want to go home. Where can I get some breakfast?"

"Dunno," said the boy. "Have some of these?"

He took a handful of acorns from a dirty satchel, and held them out, Robin catching at them eagerly, putting one between his white teeth, and biting it, but only to make a face full of disgust.

"It's bitter," he said. "It's not good to eat."

"Makes our tigs fat," said the boy; "look at 'em."

"But I'm not a pig," said Robin. "I want some bread and milk. Where can I get some?"

The boy shook his head.

"Where do you live?" asked Robin.

"Along o' master."

"Where's that?"

The boy shook his head and stared at the cap and feather, one of his hands opening and shutting.

"Will you show me the way home, then?"

The boy shook his head again, and now stared at the velvet jerkin, then at his own garb, which consisted of a piece of sack with slits in it for his head and arms to come through, and a strip of cow-skin for a belt to hold it in.

"I could show you where to get something," he said at last.

"Well, show me," cried Robin.

"You give me that jacket and cap, then," cried the boy, in a husky, low voice.

"Give you my clothes?" said Robin, wonderingly. "I can't do that."

"Then I shall take 'em?" said the boy, in a husky growl.

"I'm so hungry," cried Robin. "Show me where to get something, and I'll give you my cap and feather."

"I wants the jacket too," said the boy.

"I tell you I can't give you that," cried Robin.

"Then I means to take it."

Robin shrank away, and the boy turned upon him fiercely.

"None of that," he cried. "See this here stick? If you was to try to run away I should send it spinning after you, and it would break your legs and knock you down, and I could send the tigs after you, and they'd soon bring you back."

Robin drew a deep breath; he felt hot, and his hands clenched as he longed to strike out at his tyrant. But the young swineherd was big and strong, and the little fellow knew that he could do next to nothing against such an enemy.

Then there was a pause. Robin stood, hot, excited, and panting; the herd-boy threw himself down on his chest, rested his chin upon his hands, as he stared fiercely at Robin, and kicked his feet up and down; while the pigs roamed here and there, nuzzling the fallen acorns out from the bracken, and crunching them up loudly.

Robin wanted to run, and he did not want to run, and all at the same time, for his strongest desire just then was to fight his tyrant; and for some minutes neither spoke.

At last the big boy said, in a low, growling way:

"Now then, are you going to give me them things?"

"No," said Robin, through his set teeth; and again there was silence.

"You give 'em to me, and I'll show you the way to where they live and they'll give you roast deer and roast pig p'raps, for two of ourn's gone. Master says he counted 'em, and they aren't all there, and he wales me with a strap because I let them take the pigs, and next time he counts 'em there's more than there was before, but he's whipped me all the same. You give me them things, and I'll take you where you'll get lots to eat, and milk and eggs and apples. D'yer hear?"

"I won't give them to you. I can't--I mustn't," cried Robin passionately.

The boy said nothing, but looked away at his pigs, two of which were fighting.

"Ah, would you?" he cried; and he made believe to rush at them with his big hook-handled stick.

Robin was thrown off his guard, and before he was aware of it the boy made a side leap and, dropping his stick, seized him, threw him over on his back, and sat astride upon his chest.

"Now won't you give em to me?" cried the herd-boy; and he whipped off the cap and threw it to a little distance, with the result that half a dozen pigs rushed at it; and as he made a brave fight to get rid of his enemy, the last that Robin saw of his velvet cap and plume was that one black pig tore out the feather, while another was champing the velvet in his mouth.

It was a brave fight, but all in vain, and a few minutes later the boy was standing triumphantly over poor Robin, with the gay jerkin rolled up under his arm; and the little fellow struggled to his feet in his trunk hose and white linen shirt, hot, angry, and torn, and wishing with all his might that he were as big and strong as the tyrant who had mastered him.

"I told yer I would," said the young ruffian, with a grin. "You should ha' given 'em to me at first, and then I shouldn't have hurt yer. Come on; I'll show yer now where yer can get something to eat."

In his anger and shame Robin felt that he wanted no food now, only to go and hide himself away among the trees; but his enemy's next words had their effect.

"You didn't want this here," he said. "You've got plenty on you now. Better nor I have. There, go straight on there, and I'll show yer. D'yer hear?"

"I don't want to go now," said Robin fiercely.

"Oh, don't yer? Then I do. You're agoing afore I makes yer, and when they've give yer a lot, you're going to eat part and bring some to me so's I can help eat the rest. You bring a lot, mind, 'cause I can eat ever so much. Now then, go on."

"I can't--I don't want to," cried Robin. "You go first."

"What, and master come, p'raps, and find me gone! Likely! he'd give me the strap again. There, get on."

Robin winced, for the young ruffian picked up his stick and poked him as he would one of his pigs. But the little fellow could not help himself, and he went on in the required direction among the trees, the forest growing darker and darker, till suddenly voices were heard, and the boy stopped,

"You go straight along there," he said, "and I'll wait."

"No, you go," said Robin. "You know them."

"Oh! yes, and them want some more pigs! Want me to be leathered again?"

Robin said "No," but he felt all the time that he should like to see the young tyrant flogged and forced to return the folded up doublet; and he thought sadly of his spoiled and lost cap.

CHAPTER III

N ow then, don't you be long," cried the young swineherd, and he raised his stick threateningly, and made another thrust at Robin, which was avoided; and feeling desperate now as well as hungry, feeling too, that it would be better to fall into any other hands, the little fellow ran on, following a faint track in and out among the trees, till he came suddenly into an opening, face to face with a group of fifty or sixty people busily engaged around a heap beneath a spreading beech tree.

Robin's first act was to stand and stare, for the heap consisted of bales similar to those with which he had seen the mules laden a couple of days back, and tied up together a few yards away were the very mules, while the little crowd of men who were busy bore a very strong resemblance to those by whom the attack was made on the previous day.

Robin knew nothing in those days about the old proverb of jumping out of the frying-pan into the fire, but he felt something of the kind as he found himself face to face with the marauders who had seized upon the bales of cloth and put his aunt's servants to flight, and without a moment's hesitation he turned and began to hurry back, but ran into the arms of a huge fellow who caught him up as if he had been a baby.

"Hullo, giant!" cried the big man, "who are you?" And the party of men with him, armed with long bows and arrows, began to laugh merrily.

"Let me go--let me go!" cried the boy, struggling angrily.

"Steady, steady, my little Cock Robin," said the man, in his big bluff way; "don't fight, or you'll ruffle your feathers."

The boy ceased struggling directly.

"How did you know my name was Robin?" he said.

"Guessed it, little one. There, I shan't hurt you. Where do you come from?"

"Ellton," said the boy.

"But what are you doing here in the forest?"

"You came and fought David, and frightened him and the men away, and those are our mules and the cloth."

Robin stopped short, for the big man broke out into a loud whistle, and then laughed.

"Oh, that's it, is it?" he said; "and so your name's Robin, is it?"

The little fellow nodded. "Yes," he said. "What's yours?"

"John," said the great fellow, laughing heartily; "and they call me little because I'm so big. What do you think of that?"

"I think it's very stupid," said the boy. "I thought you must be Robin Hood."

"Then you thought wrong. But if you thought that this one was you would be right. Here he comes." The boy looked in wonder at a tall man who looked short beside Little John, as he came up in coat of green with brown belt, a sword by his side, quiver of arrows hung on his back, and longbow in his hand.

"What woodland bird have you got here, John?" he said. And the boy saw that he smiled pleasantly and did not look fierce or threatening.

"A young Robin," said the big fellow; "part of yesterday's plunder."

"I want to find my way home," said the boy. "Will you please show me?"

"But you did not come here into the forest in shirt and hose, did you, my little man?" said the great outlaw.

"No; someone took my cap and doublet away, sir."

Robin Hood frowned.

"Who was it?" he cried angrily. "Find out, John, and he shall have a bowstring about his back. Point out the man who stripped you, my little lad," he continued, turning to the boy.

"It wasn't a man," said the little fellow, "but a boy who minds pigs."

"What, a young swineherd!" cried the outlaw, laughing. "Why did you let him? Why didn't you fight for your clothes like a man?"

"I did," said young Robin stoutly; "but he was so big, he knocked me down and sat upon me."

"Oh! that makes all the difference. How big was he--big as this man?"

Young Robin glanced at the giant who had caught him, and shook his head.

"No," he said; "not half, so big as he is. But he was stronger than I am."

"So I suppose. Well, bring him along. Little John, and let's see if the women can find him some clothes and a cap. You would like something more to wear, wouldn't you?"

"I should like something to eat,'" said the boy sadly. "I have not had anything since breakfast."

"That's not so very long," said Robin Hood. "We have not had anything since breakfast."

"But I mean since breakfast yesterday," said young Robin piteously.

"What!" cried Little John. "Why, the poor boy's starved. But we can soon mend that. Come here!"

Young Robin's first movement was to shrink from the big fellow, but he smiled down in such a bluff, amiable way, that the boy gave him his hands, and in an instant he was swung up and sitting six feet in the air upon the great fellow's shoulder, and then rode off to an open-fronted shed-like place thatched with reeds, Robin Hood, with his bow over his shoulder, walking by the side.

"Here, Marian," cried the outlaw, and young Robin's heart gave a throb and he made a movement to get down to go to the sweet-faced woman who came hurriedly out, wide-eyed and wondering, in her green kirtle, her long soft naturally curling hair rippling down her back, but confined round her brow by a plain silver band in which a few woodland flowers were placed.

"Oh! Robin," she cried, flushing with pleasure; "who is this?"

"It is some one for you to take care of," said the outlaw, who smiled at the bright look in the girl's face. "He is both hungry and tired, and his people ran away and left him alone in the forest."

"Oh, my dear!" she cried, as Little John lightly jumped the boy down at her feet. "Come along."

Young Robin put his hand in hers and gave her a look full of trust and confidence, before turning to the two men, for all his troubles seemed over now.

"Thank you for bringing me here," he said; "but are you bold Robin Hood and Little John, of whom I've heard my father talk?"

"I daresay we are the men he has talked about," said the outlaw smiling; "but who is your father, and what did he say?"

"My father is the Sheriff of Nottingham," said the boy, "and he said that he was going to catch you and your men some day, for you were very wicked and bad. But he did not know how good and kind you are, and I shall tell him when you send me home."

The two men exchanged glances with Maid Marian.

"We shall see," said the outlaw; "but you are nearly starved, aren't you?"

"Yes, very, very hungry," said the boy, looking piteously at his new protector, whose hand he held.

"Hungry?" she cried.

"Yes, he has had nothing since yesterday morning; but you can cure that."

"Oh, my dear, my dear!" cried the woman. And she hurried young Robin beneath the shelter, and in a very short time he was smiling up in her face in his thankfulness, for she had placed before him a bowl of sweet new milk and some of the nicest bread he had ever tasted.

As he ate hungrily he had to answer Maid Marian's questions about who he was and how he came there, which he did readily, and it did not strike him as being very dreadful that the mules and their loads had been seized, for old David had been very cross and severe with him for getting tired, and these people in the forest were most kind.

CHAPTER IV

It was a very strange life for a boy who had been accustomed to every comfort, but young Robin enjoyed it, for everything seemed to be so new and fresh, and the men treated him as if he had come to them for the purpose of being made into a pet.

They were, of course, fierce outlaws and robbers, ready to turn their bows and swords against anyone; but the poor people who lived in and about the forest liked and helped them, for Robin Hood's men never did them harm, while as to young Robin, they were all eager to take him out with them and show him the wonders of the forest.

On the second day after his arrival in the camp, the boy asked when he was to be shown the way home, and he asked again on the third day, but only to be told each time that he should go soon.

On the fourth day he forgot to ask, for he was busy with big Little John, who smiled with satisfaction when young Robin chose to stay with him instead of going with some of the men into the forest after a deer.

Young Robin forgot to ask when he was to be shown the way home, because Little John had promised to make him a bow and arrows and to teach him how to use them. The great tall outlaw kept his word too, and long before evening he hung a cap upon a broken bough of an oak tree and set young Robin to work about twenty yards away shooting arrows at the mark.

"You've got to hit that every time you shoot," said Little John; "and when you can do that at twenty yards you have got to do it at forty. Now begin."

For the bow was ready and made of a piece of yew, and half a dozen arrows had been finished.

"Think you can hit it?" said Little John, after showing the boy how to string his bow and fit the notch of the arrow to the string.

"Oh! yes," said Robin confidently.

"That's right! then you will soon be able to kill a deer."

"But I don't want to kill a deer," said the boy. "I want to see some, but I shouldn't like to kill one."

"Wait till you're hungry, my fine fellow," said Little John, laughing. "But my word! you look fine this morning; just like one of us. Did Maid Marian make you that green jerkin?"

"Yes," said the boy.

"That's right; so's your cap and feather. But now then, try if you can hit the cap. Draw the arrow right to the head before you let it go. My word, what funny little fumbling fingers yours are!"

"Are they?" cried Robin, who thought that his teacher's hands were the biggest he had ever seen.

"Like babies' fingers," said Little John, smiling down at the boy as if very much amused. "Now then, draw right to the head."

"I can't," said the boy; "it's so hard."

"That's because you are not used to it, little one. Try again. Hold tight, and pull hard. Steadily. That's the way. Now loose it and let it go."

Young Robin did as he was told, and away went the arrow down between the trees, to fall with its feathered wings just showing above the fallen leaves.

"That didn't hit the cap," said Little John. "Never went near."

Young Robin shook his head.

"Did you look at the cap when you loosed the arrow?"

"No," said Robin; "I shut my eyes."

"Try again then, and keep them open."

Robin tried and tried again till he had sent off all six of his shafts, and then he stood and looked up at Little John, and Little John looked down at him.

"You couldn't kill a deer for dinner to-day," said the big fellow.

"No," said young Robin; "it's so hard. Could you have hit it?"

"I think I could if I stood ten times as far away," said the great fellow quietly.

"Oh, do try, please," cried Robin.

"Very well; only let's pick up your arrows first, or we may lose some of them.

Always pick up your arrows while they are fresh--I mean, while you can remember where they are."

The shafts were picked up, mostly by Little John, whose eyes were very sharp at seeing where the little arrows lay; and then they walked back, and Robin had to run by his big companion's side, for he began to stride away, counting as he went, till he had taken two hundred steps from the tree all along one of the alleys of the forest, when he stopped short.

"Now then, my little bowman," he said; "think I can hit the mark now?"

"No," said Robin decisively; "we're too far away. I can hardly see the cap."

"Well, let's try," said Little John, stringing his bow, and then carefully selecting an arrow from the quiver at his back. This arrow he drew two or three times through his hand so as to smooth the feathering and make the web lie straight, before fitting the notch to the string.

"So you think it's too far?" said Little John.

"Yes, ever so much."

"Ah, well, we'll try," said the big fellow coolly. "Where-about shall I hit the cap--in the middle?"

"No," said Robin; "just at the top of the brim."

"Very well," said the big fellow, standing up very straight and rather sidewise, as he held his bow at his left arm's length, slowly drew the arrow to the head, and then as Robin gazed in the direction of the indistinctly seen hat hanging on the tree-trunk--

Twang!

The arrow had been loosed, and the bow had given forth a strange deep musical sound.

Robin looked sharply at Little John, and the big outlaw looked down at him.

"Where did that arrow go?" said the boy.

"Let's see," said Little John.

"I don't think we shall ever find it again," continued Robin.

They walked back, the outlaw very slowly, and Robin quite fast so as to keep up with him.

"Perhaps not," said Little John, "but I don't often lose my arrows."

"This one has gone right through the ferns," thought Robin, and he felt glad with the thought of the big fellow having missed the mark, but as they walked nearer, he kept his eyes fixed upon the great trunk dimly seen in the shade, being tripped up twice by the bracken fronds; but he saved himself from a fall and watched the tree trunk still, while the hat hanging on the old bough grew plainer, just as it had been before.

They had walked back nearly three parts of the way when Robin suddenly saw something which made him start, for there was a tiny bit of something white above something dark, and those marks were not on the brim of the hat before.

The next minute Robin's eyes began to open wider, for he knew that he was looking at the feathered end of the arrow, pointing straight at him; and directly after, as he stepped a little on one side to avoid an ant-hill, he could see the whole of the arrow except the point, which had passed through the brim of the hat.

"Why, you hit it!" he cried excitedly.

"Well, that's what I tried to do," said Little John.

"But you hit it just in the place I said."

"Yes, you told me to," said Little John, smiling. "That's how you must learn to shoot when you grow up to be a man."

Young Robin said nothing, but stood rubbing one ear very gently, and staring at the hat.

"Well," said Little John, smiling down at his companion, "what are you thinking about?"

"I was thinking that it is very wonderful for you to stand so far off and shoot like that."

"Were you, now?" said Little John. "Well, it is not wonderful at all. If you keep on trying for years you will be able to do it quite as well. I'll teach you. Shall I?"

"I should like you to," said Robin, shaking his head; "but I can't stop here. I must go home to my father."

"Oh! must you?" said Little John. "Go home to your father and mother, eh?"

Robin shook his head.

"No," he said; "my mother's dead, and I live sometimes with father and sometimes with aunt. I am going home to father now, as soon as you show me the way. When are you going to show me?"

Little John screwed up his face till it was full of wrinkles. "Ah," he said, "I don't know. You must ask the captain."

"Who is the captain?" said the boy.

"Eh? Why, Robin Hood, of course. But I wouldn't ask him just yet."

"Why not?"

"Eh? Why not? Because it might be awkward. You see, it's a long way, and you couldn't go by yourself."

"Well, you could show me," said young Robin. "You would, wouldn't you?"

"I would if I could," said Little John; "but I'm afraid I couldn't."

"Oh! you could, I'm sure," said young Robin. "You're so big."

"Oh! yes, I'm big enough," said Little John, laughing; "but if I were to take you home your father would not let me come back again; and besides, the captain would not let me go for fear that I should be killed."

"Killed?" said the boy, staring at his big companion.

"Why, who would kill you?"

"Your father, perhaps."

"What, for being kind to me?"

"I can't explain all these things to you, mite. Here's someone coming. Let's ask him. Hi! Captain! Young squire wants me to take him home."

Robin Hood, who had just caught sight of the pair and come up, smiled and shook his head.

"Not yet, little one," he said. "I can't spare big Little John. Why, aren't you happy here in the merry greenwood under the trees? I thought you liked us."

"So I do," said young Robin, "and I should like to stay ever so long and watch the deer and the birds, and learn to shoot with my bow and arrows."

"That's right. Well said, little one," cried Robin Hood, patting the boy on the head.

"But I'm afraid that my father will be very cross if I don't try to go home."

"Then try and make yourself happy, my boy," said Robin Hood, "for you have tried hard to go home, and you cannot go."

"Why?" said young Robin.

"For a dozen reasons," said the outlaw, smiling. "Here are some: you could not find your way; you would starve to death in the forest; you might meet people who would behave worse to you than the young swineherd, or encounter wild beasts;

then, biggest reason of all: I will not let you go."

Young Robin was silent for a moment or two, and then he said quickly:

"You might tell Little John to take me home. My father would be so glad to see him."

Robin Hood and the big fellow just named looked at one another and laughed.

"Yes," said Robin Hood, patting the boy on the shoulder, "now that's just it. Your father, the Sheriff, would be so glad to see Little John that he would keep him altogether; and I can't spare him."

"I don't think my father would be so unkind," said Robin.

"But I am sure he would, little man," said the outlaw. "He'd be so glad to get him that he would spoil him. Eh, John? What do you think?"

"Ay, that he would," said Little John, shaking his head. "He'd be sure to spoil me. He'd cut me shorter, perhaps, or else hang me up for an ornament. No, my little man, I couldn't take you home."

"There," said the outlaw, smiling; "you must wait, my boy. Try and be contented as you are. Maid Marian's very kind to you, is she not?"

"Oh! yes," cried the boy, with his face lighting up, "and that's why I don't want to go."

"Hullo!" growled Little John. "Why, you said just now that you did want to go!" "Did I?" said the boy thoughtfully.

"To be sure you did. What do you mean."

"I mean," said the boy, looking wistfully from one to the other, "that I feel as if I ought to go home, but I think I should like to stay."

"Hurrah!" cried Little John, taking off and waving his hat. "Hear that, captain? You've got another to add to your merry men. Young Robin and I make a capital pair. Come along, youngster, and let's practise shooting at the mark, and then we'll make enough arrows to fill your quiver."

Five minutes later young Robin was standing as he had been placed by his big companion, who sat down and watched him while he sturdily drew the notch of his arrow right to his ear, and then loosed the whizzing shaft to go flying away through the woodland shade, while Little John shouted as gleefully as some big boy.

"Hurrah! Well done, little one! There it is, sticking in yonder tree."

CHAPTER V

As far as you like, Robin," said the outlaw, "only you must be wise. Don't go far enough to lose your way. Learn the forest by degrees. Some day you will not be able to lose yourself."

"But suppose I did lose myself," said the boy; "what then?"

"I should have to tell Little John to bring all my merry men to look for you, and Maid Marian here would sit at home and cry till you were found."

"Then I will not lose myself," said Robin. And he always remembered his promise when he took his bow and arrows and, with his sword hanging from his belt, went away from the outlaws' camp for a long ramble.

His bow was just as high as he was himself, that being the rule in archery, and his arrows, beautifully made by Little John, were just half the length of his bow.

As to his sword, that was a dagger in a green shark-skin sheath given to him by Robin Hood, who said rightly enough that it was quite big enough for him.

Maid Marian found a suitable buckle for the belt, one which Little John cut out of a very soft piece of deer-skin, the same skin forming the cross-belt which went over the boy's shoulder and supported his horn.

For he was supplied with a horn as well, this being necessary in the forest, and Robin Hood himself taught him in the evenings how to blow the calls by fitting his lips to the mouthpiece and altering the tone by placing his hand inside the silver rim which formed the mouth.

It was not easy, but the little fellow soon learned. All the same, though, he made some strange sounds at first, bad enough, Little John declared, to give one of Maid Marian's cows the tooth-ache, and frighten the herds of deer farther and farther away.

That was only at the first, for young Robin very soon became quite a woodman, learning fast to sound his horn, to shoot and hit his mark, and to find his way through the great wilderness of open moorland and shady trees.

But it was more than once that he lost his way, for the trees and beaten tracks were so much alike and all was so beautiful that it was easy to wander on and forget all about finding the way back through the sun-dappled shades.

And so it happened that one morning when the outlaw band had gone off hunting, to bring back a couple of fat deer for Robin Hood's larder, young Robin started by himself, bow in hand, down one of the lovely beech glades, and had soon gone farther than he had been before.

The squirrels dropped the beech mast and dashed away through the trees, to chop and scold at him; the rabbits started from out of the ferns and raced away fast, showing the under part of their white cotton tails, before they plunged into their shady burrows; and twice over, as the boy softly passed out of the shade into some sunny opening, he came upon little groups of deer--beautiful large-eyed thin-legged does, with their fawns--grazing peacefully on the soft grass which grew in patches between the tufts of golden prickly furze, for they were safe enough, the huntsmen being gone in search of the lordly bucks, with their tall flattened horns if they were fallow deer, small, round, and sharply pointed if they were roes.

There was always something fresh to see, and he who went slowly and softly through the forest saw most. At such times as this young Robin would stop short to watch the grazing deer and fawns with their softly dappled hides, till all at once a pair of sharp blue eyes would spy him out, and the jay who owned those eyes would set up his soft speckled crest, show his fierce black moustachios, and shout an alarm again in a harsh voice--"Here's a boy! here's a boy!" and the does would leave off eating, throw up their heads, and away the little herd would go, nip--nip--nip, in a series of bounds, just as if their thin legs were so many springs, their black hoofs coming down close together and just touching the short elastic grass, which seemed to send them off again.

"I wish they wouldn't be afraid of me," young Robin said. "I shouldn't hurt them."

But the does and fawns did not know that, for as Robin said this he was fitting an arrow to his bow-string, and threatening to send it flying after the shrieking jay which had given the alarm. He forgot, too, that he had eaten heartily of delicious roasted fawn only a few days before.

As he wandered on through glades where the sun seemed to send rays of glowing silver down through the oak or beech leaves as if to fill the golden cups which grew beneath them among the soft green moss, he would come out suddenly perhaps on one of the sunny forest pools, perhaps where the water was half covered with broad flat leaves, among which were silver blossoms, in other places golden, with arrow weed at the sides, along with whispering reeds and sword-shaped iris plants. There beneath the floating leaves great golden-sided carp and tench floated, and sometimes a fierce-eyed green-splashed pike, while over all flitted and darted upon gauzy wings beautiful dragon-flies, chasing the tiny gnats--blue, brown, golden, and golden-green--and now and then encountering and making their wings rustle as they touched in rapid flight. Then as he stood with his hand resting against a tree trunk, peering forward, a curious little head with bright crimson eyes divided the sedge or reeds growing in the water, its owner looking out to see if there was any danger; and as it looked, Robin could see that the bird's beak seemed to be continued right up into a fiat red plate between its eyes.

Then it came sailing out, swimming by means of its long thin legs and toes, coming right into the opening, looking of a dark shiny brownish green, all but its stunted tail, the under part of which was pure white, with a black band across.

Little John told him afterwards that it was a moor-hen, even if it was a cock bird. It was, not this which took so much of Robin's attention, but the seven or eight little dark balls which followed it out along one of the lanes of open water, swimming here and there and making dabs with their little beaks at the insects gliding about the top.

It was so quiet and seemed so safe that directly after the reeds parted again and another bird swam out from among the sheltering reeds. Robin knew this directly as a drake, but he had never before seen one with such a gloriously green head, rich chestnut-colored breast, soft gray back, or glistening metallic purple wing spots.

Robin could have sent a sharp-pointed arrow at this beautiful bird, and perhaps have killed it, for he knew well that roast duck or drake is very nice stuffed with sage and onions, and with green peas to eat therewith; but he never thought of using his bow, and he was content to feast his eyes upon the bird's beauty and watch its motions.

The drake took no notice of the moor-hen and her dusky dabs, but swam right out in the middle, seemed to stand up on the water, stretching out his neck and flapping his wings so sharply that something right on the other side moved suddenly, and Robin saw that there was another bird which he had not seen before--a long-necked, long-legged, loose-feathered gray creature with sharp eyes and a thin beak, standing in the water and staring eagerly at the drake as much as to say:

"What's the matter there?" while he uttered aloud the one enquiring cry--"Quaik?"

"Wirk--wirk--wirk!" said the drake.

"Quack, quack, quack, quack!" came from out of the reeds, and a brown duck came sailing out, followed by ten little yellow balls of down with flat beaks, swimming like their mother, but in a hurried pop-and-go-one fashion, in and out, and round and round, and seeming to go through country dances on the water in chase of water beetles and running spiders or flies, while the duck kept on uttering a warning quack, and the drake, who, first with one eye and then with the other, kept a sharp look up in the sky for falcons and hawks, now and then muttered out a satisfied "Wirk--wirk--wirk!"

Robin was Just thinking how beautiful it all was, when the danger for which the drake was watching in the sky suddenly came from the water beneath.

One of the downy yellow dabs had swum two yards away from the others and his mother, after a daddy long-legs which had flown down on to the surface of the water, and had opened its little flat beak to seize it, when there was a whirl in the water, a rush and splash, and two great jaws armed with sharp teeth closed over the duckling, which was visible one moment, gone the next, and Robin drew an arrow out to fit to his bow-string.

But he was too late to send it whizzing at the great pike, which had given a whisk with its tail and gone off to some lair in the reeds to peacefully swallow the young duck, while the rest followed their quacking father and mother back to the shelter of the reeds, rushes, and sedge, where the moor-hen and her brood were already safe, while, startled by the alarm, the heron bent down as it spread its great gray wing's, sprang up, gave a few flaps and flops, and began to sail round above the pool till it grew peaceful again, when, stretching out its legs, the heron dropped back into the water, stood motionless gazing down with meditative eyes as if quite satisfied that no fish would touch it, and then, *flick*!

It had taken place so rapidly that Robin hardly saw the movement, but certainly the heron's beak was darted in amongst the bottoms of the reeds where they grew out of the water, and directly afterwards the bird straightened itself again, to stand up with a kicking green frog in its scissor-shaped beak.

Then there was a jerk or two, which altered the frog's position, and the beak from being only a little way open was shut quite close, and a knob appeared in the heron's long neck, went slowly lower and lower, and then disappeared altogether.

Then the heron shuffled its wings a little as if to put the feathers quite straight, said "Phenk" loudly twice over, and shut one eye.

For the bird had partaken of a satisfactory dinner, and was thinking about it, while young Robin sighed and thought it seemed very dreadful; but the next moment he was watching a streak of blue, which was a kingfisher with a tiny silver fish in its beak, and thinking he was beginning to feel hungry himself.

So he left the side of the pool with another sigh, the noise he made sending off the great gray heron, and after a little difficulty he found his way back to the outlaws' camp and his own dinner, which, oddly enough, was not roast buck or fawn, but roast ducks and a fine baked pike, cooked in an earthen oven, with plenty of stuffing.

Then, being hungry, young Robin partook of his own meal, and forgot all about what he had seen.

CHAPTER VI

It was all very wonderful to young Robin when he saw Little John or one of the other men let fly an arrow with a twang of the bow-string and a sharp whizz of the wings through the air, to quiver in a mark eighty or a hundred yards away, or to pierce some flying wild goose or duck passing in a flock high in air; but by degrees that which had seemed so marvellous soon ceased to astonish him, and at last looked quite easy.

For Robin was delighted with his bow and arrows as soon as he found that he could send one of the light-winged shafts whistling in a beautiful curve to stick in some big tree.

Then he began shooting at smaller trees, and then at saplings when he could hit the small trees. But the saplings were, of course, much more difficult. One day though, he went back to Little John in triumph to tell him that he had shot at a young oak about as thick as his wrist.

"But you didn't hit it?" said the big fellow, smiling.

"I just scratched one side of it though," cried the boy.

"Did you now? Well done! You keep on trying, and you'll beat me some day."

"I don't think I shall," said Robin, shaking his head thoughtfully.

"Oh! but you will if you keep on trying. A lad who tries hard can do nearly anything."

"Can he?" said Robin.

"To be sure he can; so you try, and when you can hit anything you shoot at you'll be half a man. And when you've done growing you'll be one quite."

"Shall I ever be as big as you?" asked Robin.

"I hope not," said Little John, laughing. "I'm too big."

"Are you?" said Robin. "I should like to be as big as you."

"No, no, don't," cried Little John. "You go on growing till you're a six-footer, and then you stop. All that grows after that's waste o' good stuff, and gets in your way. Big uns like me are always knocking their heads against something."

"But how am I to know when I'm six feet high?" said Robin.

"Oh! I'll tell you, I'll keep measuring you, my lad."

"And how am I to stop growing?"

Little John took off his cap and scratched his head, as he wrinkled up his big, good-humored face.

"Well, I don't quite know," he said; "but there's plenty o' time yet, and we shall see. Might put a big stone in your hat; or keep you in a very dry place; or tie your shoulders down to your waist--no, that wouldn't do."

"Why?" said Robin promptly.

"Because it wouldn't stop your legs growing, and it's boys' legs that grow the most when they're young. I say, though, what's become of all those arrows I made you?"

"Shot them away."

"And only two left. You mustn't waste arrows like that. Why didn't you look for them after you shot?"

"I did," cried Robin, "but they will hide themselves so. They creep right under the grass and among the weeds so that you can't find them again. But you'll make me some more, won't you?"

"Well," said Little John, "I suppose I must; but you will have to be more careful, young un. I can't spend all my time making new arrows for you. But there, I want you to shoot so that the captain will be proud of you, and some day you'll have to shoot a deer."

"I don't think I should like to shoot a deer," said the boy, shaking his head.

"Why not?" They're good to eat."

"They look so nice and kind, with their big soft eyes."

"Well, a man then."

"Oh, no! I shouldn't like to shoot a man."

"What not one of the captain's enemies who had come to kill him?"

"I don't think I should mind so much then. Look here, Little John, I'd shoot an arrow into his back, to prick him and make him run away."

"And so you shall, my lad," cried Little John, and he set to work directly to cut some wood for arrows to refill the boy's quiver; and when those were lost, he made some more, for young Robin was always shooting and losing them; but Little John said it did not matter, for he was going to be a famous marksman, and the big fellow looked as proud of his pupil as could be.

But Little John did not stop at teaching young Robin to shoot, for one day the boy found him smoothing and scraping a nice new piece of ash as thick as his little finger, which was not little at all.

"You don't know what this is for," said the big fellow.

"It looks like a little quarter-staff," said young Robin, "like all the men have."

"Well done. Guessed it first time. Now guess who it is for?"

"Me," said the boy promptly. And so it was, and what was more, Little John, in the days which followed, taught him how to handle it so as to give blows and guard himself, till the little fellow became as clever and active as could be, making the men roar with laughter when in a bout he managed to strike so quickly that his staff struck leg or arm before his opponent could guard.

"Why, you're getting quite a forester, Robin," said the captain, smiling, "and what with your skill with bow and quarter-staff you'll soon be able to hold your own."

Robin Hood's words were put to the proof in autumn, for one day when the acorns had swollen to such a size that they could no longer sit in their cups, and came rattling down from the sunny side of the great oak-trees, young Robin was having a glorious ramble. He had filled his satchel with brown hazel nuts, had a good feast of blackberries, and stained his fingers. He had had a long talk to a tame fawn which knew him and came when he whistled, and tempted a couple of squirrels down with some very brown nuts, laying them upon the bark of a fallen tree, and then drawing back a few yards, with the result that the bushy-tailed little animals crept softly down, nearer and nearer, ending by making a rush, seizing the nuts, and darting back to the security of a high branch of a tree.

"I shouldn't hurt you," said Robin, as he stood leaning upon his little quarter-staff, watching them nibble away the ends of the nuts to get at the sweet kernel. "If I wanted to I could unsling my bow, string it, and bring you down with an arrow;

but I don't want to. Why can't you both be as tame as my fawn?"

The squirrels made no answer, but went on nibbling the nuts, and suddenly darted up higher in the tree, while Robin grew so much interested in the movements of the active little creatures that he heard no sound behind him, nor did he awaken to the fact that he was being stalked by some one creeping bare-footed from tree to tree to get within springing distance, till all at once he felt the whole weight of something alighting on his back and driving him forward so that he dropped his quarter-staff and came down on hands and knees.

"Got yer, have I, at last?" cried a familiar voice, as he felt his ribs nipped, his assailant having seated himself on his back. "Didn't I tell yer I'd wait, and you was to bring me back a lot to eat?"

Young Robin waited for no more, but in his agony of spirit he gave himself a wrench sidewise, dislodging his rider, and made an effort to struggle up again.

But his old enemy held fast, and after a sharp struggle Robin stood panting, face to face with the young swineherd, who had him tightly by the doublet with both hands.

"You let go," cried young Robin fiercely. "You'll tear my coat."

"I means to tear it right off dreckly," said the boy, grinning. "I want a noo un again, and it'll just do. I'm a-going to have them bow and arrows too, and the knife and cap, I'll let you see! Going and hiding away all this time, when I told yer to come back!"

"You let me go," panted Robin, looking vainly round for help.

"Nay, there aren't no one a-nigh, and I've got yer fast. Why didn't yer come back as I told you?"

"I didn't want to," said Robin angrily. "You let me go. I'll call Little John to you."

"Call him, and I'll knock his ugly old eye out," cried the boy. "I don't care for no Little Johns. I've got you now, and I'm going to pay you for not coming back before. And I know," he snarled, "you're a thief; that's what you are."

"I'm not," cried Robin fiercely, and he made a desperate struggle to get away to where his little quarter-staff lay half hidden amongst the bracken. "You let me go." But his efforts to get free were vain.

"Yes, I'll let you go, p'raps, when I've done with you and got all I wants," said the boy, in a husky, satisfied tone, as he seemed to gloat over his victim. "No, I won't; you're a thief, and a deer-stealer, and I shall just take yer to one of the King's keepers."

Young Robin set his teeth and made another struggle, but quite in vain, for he was no match in strength for his adversary.

"What! Hold still! Wo ho, kicker! Quiet, will yer!" snarled the boy. "If yer don't leave off I'll drag yer through all the worst brambles and pitch yer to my tigs. D'yer hear?" he shouted.

Robin paused breathlessly, and stood gazing wildly at his enemy.

"Yer thought I was giving yer up, did yer, but I wasn't. I've been watching for yer ever since yer run away. I knowed I should ketch yer some day. Errrr! yer young thief!"

He tightened his grip of Robin's shoulders, grinned at him like an angry dog, and gave him a fierce shake, while his victim breathed hard as he pressed his teeth together, and there was the look in his eyes as if he were some newly captured wild creature seeking a way to escape.

"Kerm along," snarled the young swineherd. "I dropped my staff just back here, and as soon as I gets it, I'm going to stand over yer while yer strips off all them things; and if yer tries to get away I'll break yer legs, and yer can't run then."

Robin drew a breath which sounded like a deep sigh, and ceased his struggling, letting his enemy force him to walk backward among the bracken and nearly fall again and again, till all at once the savage young lout shouted:

"Ah, here it is'" and loosening one hand, he was in the act of stooping to pick up the staff he had dropped in leaping upon his victim, who now made a bound which sent the boy face downward on to his staff, while Robin dashed off to where his own quarter-staff lay among the bracken--a spot he had glanced at again and again.

He seized it in an instant, and was about to bound away among the trees, but his enemy had recovered himself, and staff in hand, came after him at so terrible a rate that Robin only avoided a swishing blow at his legs by dodging round a tree, which received the stroke.

The next moment Robin faced round in the open beyond the tree, and stood on guard as he had been taught.

"Ah, would yer?" snarled the young swineherd; "take that then."

Whisk went the staff and then crack as it was received by Robin across his own, and then, profiting by Little John's lessons, he brought his own over from the left and delivered a sounding blow on his assailant's head.

The swineherd uttered a savage yell as he staggered back, but came fiercely on again, striking with all his might, but so wildly that Robin easily avoided the blow, and brought his own staff down whack, crash, on his enemy's shoulders, producing a couple more yells of pain. From that moment Robin had it all his own way, for he easily guarded himself from the swineherd's fierce strokes and retorted with swinging blows on first one arm, then on the other. Then he brought his staff down with a blow beside his enemy's left leg, then half behind the right, making him dance and limp as he yelled and sought in vain to beat down his active little adversary, who delivered a shower of cleverly directed blows in response to the wild swoops given with the worst of aim.

In the heat and excitement Robin had felt no fear. He was on his mettle, and fighting for liberty, to gain which he felt that he must effectually beat his enemy; and thanks to Little John's lessons he thrashed him so well that at the end of five minutes the young swine-herd received a final stroke across the knuckles which made him shriek, drop his staff, and turn to run down a long straight avenue in the forest where the ground was open.

Robin in his excitement began to run after him to continue the beating, but the swineherd went too fast, and on the impulse of the moment the victor stopped short, dropping his own staff and unslinging his bow from where it hung. In less time than it takes to tell the bow was strung and an arrow fitted, drawn to the head, and with a twang it was loosed after the flying lad, now a hundred yards away; but as soon as it was shot Robin repented.

"It'll kill him," he thought, and his heart seemed to stand still.

For the boy's teacher had taught well, and here was the proof. Truly as if a long careful aim had been taken the arrow sped many times faster than the swineherd ran, and Robin's eyes dilated as he saw his adversary give a sudden spring and fall upon his face, uttering a hideous yell.

Robin, full of repentance, started off to his enemy's help, but before he had gone many yards the swineherd sprang up and began to run faster than ever, while when Robin reached the spot there lay his arrow, but the lad was gone.

"Only pricked him a bit," said Little John, when he heard of the adventure. "Serve the young wretch right. But the quarter-staff. My word, big un, I'd have given something to have been there to hear his bones rattle. Well, I didn't teach you for naught. But look here, if you meet that fellow in the forest again don't you wait for him to begin; you go at him at once."

Robin nodded his head, but he never saw the swineherd again.

CHAPTER VII

Young Robin's father, the Sheriff, suffered very sadly from the loss of his son and his goods, and Robin's aunt came to Nottingham and wept bitterly over the loss of the little boy she loved dearly. For David, the old servant in whose charge Robin had been placed when he was going home, had done what too many weak people do, tried to hide one fault by committing another.

Robin was given into his charge to protect and take safely home to his father, and when the attack was made by the outlaw's men, instead of doing anything to protect the little fellow and save him from being injured by Robin Hood's people, he thought only of himself. He threw his charge into the first bushes he came to, and galloped away, hardly stopping till he reached Nottingham town.

There the first question the Sheriff asked was, not what had become of the pack mules and the consignment of cloth, but where was Robin, and the false servant said that he had fought hard to save him in the fight, but fought in vain, and that the poor boy was dead.

And then months passed and a year had gone by, and people looked solemn and said that it seemed as if the Sheriff would never hold up his head again. But they thought that he should have gathered together a number of fighting men and gone and punished Robin Hood and his outlaws for carrying off that valuable set of loads of cloth.

But Robin's father cared nothing for the cloth or the mules; he could only think of the bright happy little fellow whom he loved so well, and whom he wept for in secret at night when there was no one near to see.

Robin's aunt when she came and tried to comfort him used to shake her head and wipe her eyes. She said little, only thought a great deal, and she came over again and again to try and comfort her dead sister's husband; but it made no difference, for the Sheriff was a sadly altered man.

Then all at once there was a change, and it was at a time when Robin's aunt was over to Nottingham.

For one day a man came to the Sheriff's house and wanted him. But the Sheriff would not see him, for he took no interest in anything now, and told his servant that the man must send word what his business was.

The servant went out, and came back directly.

"He says, sir, that he was taken prisoner by Robin Hood's men a week ago, and that he has just come from the camp under the greenwood tree, and has brought you news, master."

The Sheriff started up, trembling, and told his servant to bring the strange man in.

It was no beaten and wounded ruffian, but a hale and hearty fellow, who looked bright and happy, and before he could speak and tell his news the Sheriff began to question him.

"You have come from the outlaws' camp?" he said with his voice trembling.

"Yes, Master Sheriff."

"They took you prisoner, and beat and robbed you?"

"Oh! no, Master Sheriff; they took me before Robin Hood, and he asked me what I was doing there, and whether I was not afraid to cross his forest, and I up and told him plainly that I wasn't. Then he said how was that when I must have heard what a terrible robber he was."

"Yes, yes," cried the Sheriff, "and what did you say."

"I said that I had lived about these parts all my life and I never heard that he did a poor man any harm. Then he laughed, and all his people laughed too, and he said I was a merry fellow. 'Give him plenty to eat and drink,' he said, 'for two or three days, and then send him on his way.' Yes, Master Sheriff, that he did, and a fine jolly time I had. Why, I almost felt as if I should like to stay altogether."

And all this time the Sheriff was watching the man very keenly, and suddenly he caught him by the arm.

"Speak out," he said; "you did not come to tell me only that. What is it you are keeping back? Why don't you speak?"

"Because, master," said the man softly, "I was afraid you couldn't bear it, for I was a father once and my son died, and though you never knew me, I knew you, and was sorry when the news came that your little boy was killed. Can you bear to hear good news as well as bad?"

The Sheriff was silent for a few minutes, during which he closed his eyes and his lips moved, and he looked so strange that Robin's aunt crossed the room to where he sat, and took hold of his hand, as she whispered loving words.

"Yes, yes," he said softly, "I can bear it now. Speak, pray speak, and tell me all."

"But you will not be angry with me if I am wrong, Master Sheriff?"

"No, no," said Robin's father; "speak out at once."

"Well, Master Sheriff, no one would tell me when I asked questions, but there's a little fellow there, dressed all in Lincoln green, like one of Robin Hood's fighting men, with his sword and bugle, and bow and arrows, and somehow I began to think, and then I began to ask, whether he was Robin Hood's son; but those I asked only shook their heads.

"That made me think all the more, and one day I managed to follow him but among the trees to where I found him feeding one of the wild deer, which followed him about like a dog."

"I waited a bit, and then stepped out to him, and what do you think he did? He strung his bow, fitted an arrow to it before I knew where I was, and drew it to the head as if he was going to shoot me. 'Do you know where Nottingham is?' I said, and he lowered his bow. 'Yes,' he said, 'of course. Do you know my father?' 'Do I know the Sheriff?' I said; 'of course.' 'Are you going there soon?' he cried, and I nodded. 'Then you go to my father,' he cried, 'and tell him to tell aunt that I'm quite well, and that some day I'm coming home."

The man stopped, for just then the Sheriff closed his eyes again and said something very softly, which Robin's aunt heard, and she sank upon her knees and covered her face with her hands.

Then the Sheriff sprang to his feet, looking quite a different man.

"Here," he said to the bringer of the news, and he gave him some gold pieces. "Could you find your way back to the outlaws' camp in the forest?"

"Oh! yes, Master Sheriff, that I could, though they did bind a cloth over my face when they brought me away."

"And you could lead me and a strong body of fighting men right to the outlaws' camp?"

"I could, Master Sheriff," said the man, beginning slowly to lay the gold pieces back one by one upon the table; "but I can't do evil for good."

"What?" cried the Sheriff angrily. "They are robbers and outlaws, and every subject of the King has a right to slay them."

"May be, Master Sheriff," said the man drily; "but I'm not going to fly at the throat of one who did nothing but good to me. They tell me that Robin Hood's a noble earl who offended the King, and had to fly for his life. What I say is, he's a noble kind-hearted gentleman, and if it was my boy he had there, looking as happy as the day is long, I'd go to him without any fighting men."

"How, then?" cried the Sheriff.

"Just like a father should, master, and ask him for my boy like a man."

"That will do," said the Sheriff. "You can go."

The man turned to leave the room, when the Sheriff said sharply:

"Stop! You are leaving the gold pieces I gave you."

"Yes, I can't take pay to lead anyone to fight against Robin Hood and his men."

"Those pieces were for the news you brought me," said the Sheriff. "Yes, take them, for you have behaved like an honest man."

But the Sheriff did not take the man's advice, neither did he listen to the appeal of young Robin's aunt. For, as Sheriff of Nottingham, he said to himself that it was his duty to destroy or scatter the band of outlaws who had lived in Sherwood Forest for so long a time.

So he gathered a strong body of crossbow-men, and others with spears and swords, besides asking for the help of two gallant knights who came with their esquires mounted and in armour with their men.

Somehow Robin Hood knew what was being prepared, and about a week after, when the Sheriff and his great following of about three hundred men were struggling to make their way through the forest, they heard the sound of a horn, and all at once the thick woodland seemed to be alive with archers, who used their bows in such a way that first one, then a dozen, then by fifties, the Sheriff's men began to flee, and in less than an hour they were all crawling back to Nottingham, badly beaten, not a man among them being ready to turn and fight.

In another month the Sheriff advanced again with a stronger force, but they were driven back more easily than the first, and the Sheriff was in despair.

But a couple of days later he had the man to whom he had given the gold pieces found, and sent him to the outlaws' camp with a letter written upon parchment, in which he ordered Robin Hood, in the King's name, to give up the little prisoner he held there contrary to the law and against his own will.

It was many weary anxious days before the messenger came back, but without the little prisoner.

"What did he say?" asked the Sheriff.

"He said, master, that if you wanted the boy you must go and fetch him."

It was the very next day that the Sheriff went into the room where young Robin's aunt was seated, looking very unhappy, and she jumped up from her chair wonderingly on seeing that her brother-in-law was dressed as if for a journey, wearing no sword or dagger, only carrying a long stout walking staff.

"Where are you going, dear?" she said.

"Where I ought to have gone at first," he said humbly; "into the forest to fetch my boy."

"But you could never find your way," she said, sobbing. "Besides, you are the Sheriff, and these men will seize and kill you."

"I have someone to show me the way," said the Sheriff gently; "and somehow, though I have persecuted and fought against the people sorely, I feel no fear, for Robin Hood is not the man to slay a broken-hearted father who comes in search of his long-lost boy."

CHAPTER VIII

The sun was low down in the west, and shining through and under the great oak and beech trees, so that everything seemed to be turned to orange and gold.

It was the outlaws' supper time, the sun being their clock in the forest; and the men were gathering together to enjoy their second great meal of the day, the other being breakfast, after having which they always separated to go hunting through the woods to bring in the provisions for the next day.

Robin Hood's men, then, were scattered about under the shade of a huge spreading oak tree, waiting for the roast venison, which sent a very pleasant odor from the glowing fire of oak wood, and young Robin was seated on the mossy grass close by the thatched shed which formed the captain's headquarters, where Maid Marian was busy spreading the supper for the little party who ate with Robin Hood himself.

Little John was there, lying down, smiling and contented after a hard day's hunting, listening to young Robin, who was displaying the treasures he had brought in that day, and telling his great companion where he had found them.

There were flowers for Maid Marian, because she was fond of the purple and yellow loosestrife, and long thick reeds in a bundle.

"You can make me some arrows of those," said Robin; "and I've found a young yew tree with a bough quite straight. You must cut that down and dry it to make me a bigger bow. This one is not strong enough."

"Very well, big one," said Little John, smiling and stretching out his hand to smooth the boy's curly brown hair. "Anything else for me to do?"

"Oh yes, lots of things, only I can't think of them yet. Look here, I found these."

The boy took some round prickly husks out of his pocket.

"Chestnuts--eating ones."

"Yes, I know where you got them," said Little-John, "but they're no good. Look."

He tore one of the husks open, and laid bare the rich brown nut; but it was, as he said, good for nothing, there being no hard sweet kernel within, nothing but soft pithy woolly stuff.

"No good at all," continued the great forester; "but I'll show you a tree which bears good ones, only the nuts are better if they're left till they drop out of their husks."

"And then the pigs get them," said Robin.

"Then you must get up before the pigs, and be first. Halloa! What now?"

For a horn was blown at a distance, and the men under the great oak tree sprang to their feet, while Robin Hood came out to see what the signal meant.

Young Robin, who was now quite accustomed to the foresters' ways, caught up his bow like the rest, and stood looking eagerly in the direction from which the cheery sounding notes of the horn were blown.

He had not long to wait, for half a dozen of the merry men in green came marching towards them with a couple of prisoners, each having his hands fastened behind him with a bow-string and a broad bandage tied over his eyes, so that they should not know their way again to the outlaws' stronghold.

"Prisoners!" said young Robin.

"Poor men, too," grumbled Little John.

"Then you'll give them their supper and send them away to-morrow morning," said young Robin.

"I suppose so," said Little John, "but I don't know what made our fellows bring them in."

"Let's go and see," said young Robin.

Little John followed as the boy marched off, bow in hand, to where Robin Hood was standing, waiting to hear what his men had to say about the prisoners they had brought in. And as they drew near the boy saw that one was, a homely poor-looking man with round shoulders, the other, well dressed in sad-colored clothes, and thin and bent. But the boy could see little more for the broad bandage, which nearly covered the prisoner's face and was tied tightly behind over his long, gray hair, while his gray beard hung down low.

Young Robin looked pityingly at this prisoner, and a longing came over him to loosen the thong which tied his hands tightly behind him, and take off the bandage so that he could breathe freely, but just then Robin Hood cried:

"Well, my lads, whom have we here?"

The bowed down gray-haired prisoner rose erect at this, and cried:

"Is that Robin Hood who speaks?"

Before the outlaw could answer; he was stopped by a cry: from the boy, who threw down his bow and darted to the prisoner's side.

"Father!" he cried; and he leaped up, as active now as one of the deer of the forest, to fling his arms about the prisoner's neck.

But only for a moment.

The next he had dropped to the ground, to look fiercely round at the astonished men, as he drew the dagger which hung from his belt.

"Who dared do this?" he cried, as he reached up to tear the bandage from the face bending over him, and then darted round to begin sawing at the thong which held his father's hands.

Little John took a step or two forward to help the boy, but Robin Hood held up his hand to keep him back, and a dead silence fell upon the great group of foresters who had pressed forward, and who eagerly watched the scene before them in the soft, amber sunshine which came slanting through the trees. The task was hard, but the little fellow worked well, and many moments had not elapsed before the prisoner's hands were free, and as if seeing no one but the little forester before him in green, and quite regardless of all around, he dropped upon his knees, clasped the boy to his breast, and softly whispered the words:

"Thank God!"

Young Robin's arms were tightly round his father's neck by this time, and he was kissing the care-worn face again and again.

"They didn't know who you were, father; they didn't know who you were," cried the boy passionately, as if asking his father's pardon for the outrage committed upon him.

"No, Rob," said the Sheriff, in a choking voice; "they did not know who I was.

But you know your poor old father again."

"Know you again!" cried the boy, hanging back, and looking at his father wonderingly. "Why, yes; but what a long time you have been before you came to fetch me."

"Yes, yes, my boy; a long, long year of misery and sorrow; but I have found you now, at last."

"Oh! I am glad," cried the boy, struggling free, and catching his father's hand to lead him towards where Robin Hood and Marian were standing, wet-eyed, looking on.

"This is my father," cried the boy proudly. "This is Robin Hood, the captain, father," he continued, and the Sheriff bowed gravely; "and this is Maid Marian, who has been so good to me."

The Sheriff bowed slowly 'and gravely, as if to the greatest lady in the land, and then the boy dragged at his father's hand.

"And this is old Little John, father," he cried. "I say, isn't he big!"

The Sheriff bowed again, and the great outlaw's face wore such a comic expression of puzzlement that Robin Hood laughed aloud, and completed his great follower's confusion.

"He has been so good to me, father," cried young Robin. "I can shoot with bow and arrow now, and sound my horn. Hark!"

The boy clapped his horn to his lips and blew a few cheery notes which ran echoing down the forest glades, and the men assembled gave a hearty cheer.

"You're welcome to the woodlands, Master Sheriff," said Robin Hood, advancing now with extended hand. "Do not take this as the outlaw's hand, nor extend yours as the Sheriff; but let it be the grasp of two Englishmen, one of whom receives a guest."

"I thank you, sir," said the Sheriff slowly. "I can give you nothing but thanks, for after a year of sorrow I find my child is after all alive and well."

"And I hope not worse than when accident brought him into our hands. What do you say? Do you find him changed?"

"Bigger and stronger," said the Sheriff, drawing the boy closer to him, while the little fellow clung to his hand.

"Our woodland life; and I warrant you, Master Sheriff, that he is none the worse, for he is the truest, most gracious little fellow I ever met. Here, Little Name-sake, speak out, and let your father know you have been a good boy ever since you came here to stay."

Young Robin was silent, and looked from one to the other in a curiously abashed fashion.

"Well, boy, why don't you speak?" cried Robin Hood merrily. "I want Master Sheriff to hear that we have not spoiled you. Come, tell him. You have always been a good boy, haven't you?"

Young Robin hung his head.

"No," he said slowly, with his brow wrinkled up, his head hanging and one foot scraping softly at the mossy grass. "No, not always."

Little John burst into a tremendous roar of laughter, and began to stamp about, with the result that young Robin made a dash at him and tried vainly to climb up and clap his hand over the great fellow's lips.

"Don't--don't tell," cried the boy.

"Ran at me--only yesterday," cried Little John--"and began to thrash me in a passion."

"Don't tell tales out of school, Little John," cried Robin Hood, laughing. "There, Rob, you must forgive him; we're none of-us-perfect. Master Sheriff, and if your little fellow had been quite so, I don't think that we should all, to a man here, have loved him half so well. But come, after his confession, I think you will grant one thing, and that is, that in spite of his having spent a year in the outlaws' camp, he is as honest as the day."

"Nothing could make my boy Robin tell a lie," said the Sheriff proudly. "But, sir, I have come humbly to you now. Glad even to be your prisoner, so that I might once more see my child."

"My prisoner if you had come amongst us with your posse of armed men, sir," said Robin Hood proudly. "As it is, Master Sheriff, you come here alone with your guide, and I bid you welcome to our greenwood home. Fate made me what I am, the Sheriff's enemy, but the gentle visitor's friend. Come, Rob, my boy, show your father where he can take away the travel stains, and then bring him to our humble board."

It was the next day that was to be young Robin's last with the outlaws in the merry greenwood, and all were gathered together to bid him farewell, and see him safely with his father on the road; but not as the Sheriff had come, wearily and on foot, for half a dozen of the best mules were forthcoming, and the guests were to ride back on their journey home.

Who does not know how hard it is to say good-bye? Young Robin did not till the time had come.

He awoke that morning joyful and eager to start, for it was to go back home in company with the father whom he loved; but when the time came he had to learn how tightly so many of his little heartstrings had taken hold of the life under the greenwood tree. Everything about him had grown dear, and there was almost a mule load of treasures and pets of his own collecting that could not be left behind.

And when they had been carefully packed in panniers by Little John and one of the men, there was the task of bidding them all good-bye, and then those two words grew harder every time.

But he spoke out manfully and well, in spite of a choking sensation, till nearly the last.

"For I'm coming back again," he said, "and you'll take care of my pet fawn for me, Little John, and always remember to feed it well. And don't forget the dog and that dormouse we couldn't find, so that I can have it when I come back, and--"

Croak!

What was that?

It was a peculiar sound made up in the air by Little John, and that did it, for when young Robin looked up in astonishment, it was to see the great fellow's face all puckered up, and--yes, there were two great tears rolling down his cheeks as he caught the boy in his arms and kissed him.

And so it was that when young Robin ran to bid Maid Marian good-bye, he could no longer hold it back. As he clasped his arms about her neck, and kissed her passionately again and again, the sobs came fast, but the word *Good-bye* would not come at all, and when they rode away, the boy dared not look back for fear the men should see his red and swollen eyes. So he only waved his hat, and kept waving it to the last.

But he was to see some of his friends again, for about a year after the Sheriff of Nottingham had the strangest visitors of his life-time at his house, and young Robin enjoyed the task of welcoming them, for as one old history says, Robin Hood was forgiven and restored by the King to his rightful possessions, and then it was that he was gladly welcomed by the Sheriff, who said he was honored by the visit of the nobleman and his lady.

But it was nothing to young Robin then that his old friend was an earl, and his lady a countess; they were still Robin Hood and Maid Marian to him, and big Little John, their follower, his old friend and companion, full of memories of his year's happy life in the Merry Greenwood.

The Codes Of Hammurabi And Moses
W. W. Davies

QTY

The discovery of the Hammurabi Code is one of the greatest achievements of archaeology, and is of paramount interest, not only to the student of the Bible, but also to all those interested in ancient history...

Religion   **ISBN: *1-59462-338-4***   **Pages:132**
MSRP $12.95

The Theory of Moral Sentiments
Adam Smith

QTY

This work from 1749. contains original theories of conscience amd moral judgment and it is the foundation for systemof morals.

Philosophy **ISBN: *1-59462-777-0***   **Pages:536**
MSRP $19.95

Jessica's First Prayer
Hesba Stretton

QTY

In a screened and secluded corner of one of the many railway-bridges which span the streets of London there could be seen a few years ago, from five o'clock every morning until half past eight, a tidily set-out coffee-stall, consisting of a trestle and board, upon which stood two large tin cans, with a small fire of charcoal burning under each so as to keep the coffee boiling during the early hours of the morning when the work-people were thronging into the city on their way to their daily toil...

Childrens   **ISBN: *1-59462-373-2***   **Pages:84**
MSRP $9.95

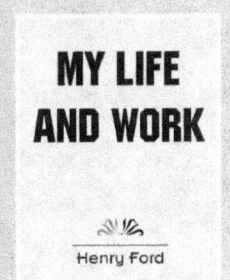

My Life and Work
Henry Ford

QTY

Henry Ford revolutionized the world with his implementation of mass production for the Model T automobile. Gain valuable business insight into his life and work with his own auto-biography... "We have only started on our development of our country we have not as yet, with all our talk of wonderful progress, done more than scratch the surface. The progress has been wonderful enough but..."

Biographies/   **ISBN: *1-59462-198-5***   **Pages:300**
MSRP $21.95

The Art of Cross-Examination
Francis Wellman

QTY

I presume it is the experience of every author, after his first book is published upon an important subject, to be almost overwhelmed with a wealth of ideas and illustrations which could readily have been included in his book, and which to his own mind, at least, seem to make a second edition inevitable. Such certainly was the case with me; and when the first edition had reached its sixth impression in five months, I rejoiced to learn that it seemed to my publishers that the book had met with a sufficiently favorable reception to justify a second and considerably enlarged edition. ..

Pages:412

Reference   ISBN: *1-59462-647-2*   *MSRP $19.95*

On the Duty of Civil Disobedience
Henry David Thoreau

QTY

Thoreau wrote his famous essay, On the Duty of Civil Disobedience, as a protest against an unjust but popular war and the immoral but popular institution of slave-owning. He did more than write—he declined to pay his taxes, and was hauled off to gaol in consequence. Who can say how much this refusal of his hastened the end of the war and of slavery ?

Law   ISBN: *1-59462-747-9*   **Pages:48**

MSRP $7.45

Dream Psychology Psychoanalysis for Beginners
Sigmund Freud

QTY

Sigmund Freud, born Sigismund Schlomo Freud (May 6, 1856 - September 23, 1939), was a Jewish-Austrian neurologist and psychiatrist who co-founded the psychoanalytic school of psychology. Freud is best known for his theories of the unconscious mind, especially involving the mechanism of repression; his redefinition of sexual desire as mobile and directed towards a wide variety of objects; and his therapeutic techniques, especially his understanding of transference in the therapeutic relationship and the presumed value of dreams as sources of insight into unconscious desires.

Pages:196

Psychology   ISBN: *1-59462-905-6*   *MSRP $15.45*

The Miracle of Right Thought
Orison Swett Marden

QTY

Believe with all of your heart that you will do what you were made to do. When the mind has once formed the habit of holding cheerful, happy, prosperous pictures, it will not be easy to form the opposite habit. It does not matter how improbable or how far away this realization may see, or how dark the prospects may be, if we visualize them as best we can, as vividly as possible, hold tenaciously to them and vigorously struggle to attain them, they will gradually become actualized, realized in the life. But a desire, a longing without endeavor, a yearning abandoned or held indifferently will vanish without realization.

Pages:360

Self Help   ISBN: *1-59462-644-8*   *MSRP $25.45*

The Rosicrucian Cosmo-Conception Mystic Christianity *by Max Heindel* ISBN: *1-59462-188-8* **$38.95**
The Rosicrucian Cosmo-conception is not dogmatic, neither does it appeal to any other authority than the reason of the student. It is: not controversial, but is: sent forth in the, hope that it may help to clear... New Age/Religion Pages 646

Abandonment To Divine Providence *by Jean-Pierre de Caussade* ISBN: *1-59462-228-0* **$25.95**
"The Rev. Jean Pierre de Caussade was one of the most remarkable spiritual writers of the Society of Jesus in France in the 18th Century. His death took place at Toulouse in 1751. His works have gone through many editions and have been republished... Inspirational/Religion Pages 400

Mental Chemistry *by Charles Haanel* ISBN: *1-59462-192-6* **$23.95**
Mental Chemistry allows the change of material conditions by combining and appropriately utilizing the power of the mind. Much like applied chemistry creates something new and unique out of careful combinations of chemicals the mastery of mental chemistry... New Age/Business Pages 354

The Letters of Robert Browning and Elizabeth Barret Barrett 1845-1846 vol II ISBN: *1-59462-193-4* **$35.95**
by Robert Browning and Elizabeth Barrett Biographies Pages 596

Gleanings In Genesis (volume I) *by Arthur W. Pink* ISBN: *1-59462-130-6* **$27.45**
Appropriately has Genesis been termed "the seed plot of the Bible" for in it we have, in germ form, almost all of the great doctrines which are afterwards fully developed in the books of Scripture which follow... Religion/Inspirational Pages 420

The Master Key *by L. W. de Laurence* ISBN: *1-59462-001-6* **$30.95**
In no branch of human knowledge has there been a more lively increase of the spirit of research during the past few years than in the study of Psychology, Concentration and Mental Discipline. The requests for authentic lessons in Thought Control, Mental Discipline and... New Age/Business Pages 422

The Lesser Key Of Solomon Goetia *by L. W. de Laurence* ISBN: *1-59462-092-X* **$9.95**
This translation of the first book of the "Lemegton" which is now for the first time made accessible to students of Talismanic Magic was done, after careful collation and edition, from numerous Ancient Manuscripts in Hebrew, Latin, and French... New Age/Occult Pages 92

Rubaiyat Of Omar Khayyam *by Edward Fitzgerald* ISBN:*1-59462-332-5* **$13.95**
Edward Fitzgerald, whom the world has already learned, in spite of his own efforts to remain within the shadow of anonymity, to look upon as one of the rarest poets of the century, was born at Bredfield, in Suffolk, on the 31st of March, 1809. He was the third son of John Purcell... Music Pages 172

Ancient Law *by Henry Maine* ISBN: *1-59462-128-4* **$29.95**
The chief object of the following pages is to indicate some of the earliest ideas of mankind, as they are reflected in Ancient Law, and to point out the relation of those ideas to modern thought. Religiom/History Pages 452

Far-Away Stories *by William J. Locke* ISBN: *1-59462-129-2* **$19.45**
"Good wine needs no bush, but a collection of mixed vintages does. And this book is just such a collection. Some of the stories I do not want to remain buried for ever in the museum files of dead magazine-numbers an author's not unpardonable vanity..." Fiction Pages 272

Life of David Crockett *by David Crockett* ISBN: *1-59462-250-7* **$27.45**
"Colonel David Crockett was one of the most remarkable men of the times in which he lived. Born in humble life, but gifted with a strong will, an indomitable courage, and unremitting perseverance... Biographies/New Age Pages 424

Lip-Reading *by Edward Nitchie* ISBN: *1-59462-206-X* **$25.95**
Edward B. Nitchie, founder of the New York School for the Hard of Hearing, now the Nitchie School of Lip-Reading, Inc, wrote "LIP-READING Principles and Practice". The development and perfecting of this meritorious work on lip-reading was an undertaking... How-to/Health Pages 400

A Handbook of Suggestive Therapeutics, Applied Hypnotism, Psychic Science ISBN: *1-59462-214-0* **$24.95**
by Henry Munro Health/New Age/Health/Self-help Pages 376

A Doll's House: and Two Other Plays *by Henrik Ibsen* ISBN: *1-59462-112-8* **$19.95**
Henrik Ibsen created this classic when in revolutionary 1848 Rome. Introducing some striking concepts in playwriting for the realist genre, this play has been studied the world over. Fiction/Classics/Plays 308

The Light of Asia *by sir Edwin Arnold* ISBN: *1-59462-204-3* **$13.95**
In this poetic masterpiece, Edwin Arnold describes the life and teachings of Buddha. The man who was to become known as Buddha to the world was born as Prince Gautama of India but he rejected the worldly riches and abandoned the reigns of power when... Religion/History/Biographies Pages 170

The Complete Works of Guy de Maupassant *by Guy de Maupassant* ISBN: *1-59462-157-8* **$16.95**
"For days and days, nights and nights, I had dreamed of that first kiss which was to consecrate our engagement, and I knew not on what spot I should put my lips..." Fiction/Classics Pages 240

The Art of Cross-Examination *by Francis L. Wellman* ISBN: *1-59462-257-9* **$26.95**
Written by a renowned trial lawyer, Wellman imparts his experience and uses case studies to explain how to use psychology to extract desired information through questioning. How-to/Science/Reference Pages 408

Answered or Unanswered? *by Louisa Vaughan* ISBN: *1-59462-248-5* **$10.95**
Miracles of Faith in China Religion Pages 112

The Edinburgh Lectures on Mental Science (1909) *by Thomas* ISBN: *1-59462-008-3* **$11.95**
This book contains the substance of a course of lectures recently given by the writer in the Queen Street Hail, Edinburgh. Its purpose is to indicate the Natural Principles governing the relation between Mental Action and Material Conditions... New Age/Psychology Pages 148

Ayesha *by H. Rider Haggard* ISBN: *1-59462-301-5* **$24.95**
Verily and indeed it is the unexpected that happens! Probably if there was one person upon the earth from whom the Editor of this, and of a certain previous history, did not expect to hear again... Classics Pages 380

Ayala's Angel *by Anthony Trollope* ISBN: *1-59462-352-X* **$29.95**
The two girls were both pretty, but Lucy who was twenty-one who supposed to be simple and comparatively unattractive, whereas Ayala was credited, as her Bombwhat romantic name might show, with poetic charm and a taste for romance. Ayala when her father died was nineteen... Fiction Pages 484

The American Commonwealth *by James Bryce* ISBN: *1-59462-286-8* **$34.45**
An interpretation of American democratic political theory. It examines political mechanics and society from the perspective of Scotsman James Bryce Politics Pages 572

Stories of the Pilgrims *by Margaret P. Pumphrey* ISBN: *1-59462-116-0* **$17.95**
This book explores pilgrims religious oppression in England as well as their escape to Holland and eventual crossing to America on the Mayflower, and their early days in New England... History Pages 268

QTY

The Fasting Cure *by Sinclair Upton*
ISBN: *1-59462-222-1* **$13.95**

In the Cosmopolitan Magazine for May, 1910, and in the Contemporary Review (London) for April, 1910, I published an article dealing with my experiences in fasting. I have written a great many magazine articles, but never one which attracted so much attention... New Age/Self Help/Health Pages 164

Hebrew Astrology *by Sepharial*
ISBN: *1-59462-308-2* **$13.45**

In these days of advanced thinking it is a matter of common observation that we have left many of the old landmarks behind and that we are now pressing forward to greater heights and to a wider horizon than that which represented the mind-content of our progenitors... Astrology Pages 144

Thought Vibration or The Law of Attraction in the Thought World
ISBN: *1-59462-127-6* **$12.95**

by William Walker Atkinson Psychology/Religion Pages 144

Optimism *by Helen Keller*
ISBN: *1-59462-108-X* **$15.95**

Helen Keller was blind, deaf, and mute since 19 months old, yet famously learned how to overcome these handicaps, communicate with the world, and spread her lectures promoting optimism. An inspiring read for everyone... Biographies/Inspirational Pages 84

Sara Crewe *by Frances Burnett*
ISBN: *1-59462-360-0* **$9.45**

In the first place, Miss Minchin lived in London. Her home was a large, dull, tall one, in a large, dull square, where all the houses were alike, and all the sparrows were alike, and where all the door-knockers made the same heavy sound... Childrens/Classic Pages 88

The Autobiography of Benjamin Franklin *by Benjamin Franklin*
ISBN: *1-59462-135-7* **$24.95**

The Autobiography of Benjamin Franklin has probably been more extensively read than any other American historical work, and no other book of its kind has had such ups and downs of fortune. Franklin lived for many years in England, where he was agent... Biographies/History Pages 332

Name	
Email	
Telephone	
Address	
City, State ZIP	

☐ **Credit Card**   ☐ **Check / Money Order**

Credit Card Number	
Expiration Date	
Signature	

Please Mail to: Book Jungle
PO Box 2226
Champaign, IL 61825
or Fax to: 630-214-0564

ORDERING INFORMATION
web*: www.bookjungle.com*
email*: sales@bookjungle.com*
fax*: 630-214-0564*
mail*: Book Jungle PO Box 2226 Champaign, IL 61825*
or PayPal *to sales@bookjungle.com*

Please contact us for bulk discounts

DIRECT-ORDER TERMS

**20% Discount if You Order
Two or More Books**
Free Domestic Shipping!
Accepted: Master Card, Visa,
Discover, American Express